HENRY and the Boy Who Thought Numbers Were Fleas

MARJORIE KAPLAN

Illustrated by HEIDI CHANG

FOUR WINDS PRESS   NEW YORK

Collier Macmillan Canada   Toronto

Maxwell Macmillan International Publishing Group
New York   Oxford   Singapore   Sydney

To David and Leslie

"Motto for a Dog House" by Arthur Guiterman
first appeared in *Wildwood Fables* and is reprinted
by permission of Louise H. Sclove.
"The Dog That Howls at Night" by Herbert J. Bryce was first published
in *The Rotarian* and appears by permission of the magazine.

Four Winds Press
Macmillan Publishing Company
866 Third Avenue, New York, NY 10022
Collier Macmillan Canada, Inc.
1200 Eglinton Avenue East, Suite 200
Don Mills, Ontario M3C 3N1
First edition
Printed in the United States of America

1   2   3   4   5   6   7   8   9   10

The text of this book is set in 12 point ITC Garamond Light.
The illustrations are rendered in pencil.
Book design by Constance Ftera

Library of Congress Cataloging-in-Publication Data
Kaplan, Marjorie.
Henry and the boy who thought numbers were fleas   /   Marjorie Kaplan;
illustrated by Heidi Chang.   —   1st ed.
p.   cm.
Summary: Henry the dog helps his owner's little brother, Sam, learn
the multiplication tables.
ISBN 0-02-749351-2
[1. Dogs—Fiction.   2. Mathematics—Fiction.]   I. Chang, Heidi,
ill.   II. Title.
PZ7.K1294He   1991   [E]—dc20   90-43852   CIP   AC

1.

Henry was a city dog who was dying to visit Indiana. He had been going to college in Chicago ever since he was a puppy, since the day that a college student named Lynn had found him shivering under a hydrangea bush on campus.

Lynn had carried Henry to class with her. He had lain so quietly next to Lynn's desk on that first day of summer school that the professors let him come every day. His favorite subjects were mathematics and poetry.

It was a good life for Henry and Lynn. After classes they'd walk home to their apartment above the Dove Restaurant on Fifty-seventh Street and eat dinner. At the end of the day, when all the books were put away, they'd watch the White Sox play baseball on television. Or, if there wasn't a game, Lynn would recite poetry to Henry.

The last thing before bed, she'd take him to the empty lot across the street from the Dove Restaurant, and he would run around with the other college dogs.

Then, when he was lying on the flowered rug next to Lynn's bed in a little shining patch of yellow from the streetlight outside their window, she would tell him about her home in Indiana.

She told him about the two big trees in the backyard. One was a willow that grew in the back corner of the yard near the fence. It had branches that came all the way down to the ground and made a wonderful hiding place. The other, her favorite, was an old maple tree.

"It's *awfully* old," Lynn said. "But so many birds build their nests in it every spring that we'd hate to chop it down."

She told him about Mom and Dad and Little Brother Sam, who was in the third grade at Happy Hollow Elementary School. Sam wanted a dog more than anything else in the world, and he was having trouble learning his times tables.

"He says if he had a dog he could learn them."

Perhaps, thought Henry. But that would depend on the dog. Not all dogs were good at arithmetic.

"I was just like Sam," Lynn said. "I dreamed about having a dog all the time. But Mom wouldn't let me have one, either."

Mom was the reason Henry hadn't been to Indiana. Mom had never really known a dog, Lynn had explained, but once, when Mom was a child, just before a 4-H fair, a stray dog had ruined her prize zucchini.

What rotten luck for a little girl, Henry had thought.

But the week before spring exams, when classes were over, Lynn decided to gather up all her books and go home to study. She called her mother. Henry was lying on the couch next to her.

"We're driving down Sunday, Mom, and we'll stay until the following Saturday."

"You're bringing the dog?" Mom asked.

Lynn tried to put the telephone very close to her ear so that Henry's feelings wouldn't be hurt. But Henry had very good ears, and he heard Mom very well.

Henry was asking himself the same question. Was he finally going to Indiana to meet Little Brother Sam and Mom and Dad?

"The girl I usually leave Henry with is going home, too. He can't take care of himself, you know. So if the dog can't come, neither can I," Lynn said.

"Then by all means bring it," Mom said. She always called Henry "it."

Henry was overjoyed. His big black tail went *thump, thump, thump, thump* against the back of the couch.

But it wasn't really true that he couldn't take care of himself. He was no longer the shivering little puppy he had been when Lynn found him nearly a year ago.

If Lynn would only leave the door to their apartment above the Dove Restaurant open a little bit, Henry could go in and out by himself. He could tip over a garbage can outside the back door of the restaurant and find good things to eat. He could run around with his friends, Prince and Junior, in the empty lot across the street. They could go along Fifty-seventh Street and sniff at the new plants coming up out of the ground. He could bum around.

Sometime that would be a fun way to spend a vacation, but Lynn would never let him stay alone in their apartment. And besides, Henry would not miss visiting Indiana for all the tidbits in the world. He wanted to hide under the willow tree. He wanted to meet Sam, and to visit Happy Hollow Elementary School.

Henry had had a year of college, but he had never been in the third grade. He was very curious about what went on there. Why, he wondered, couldn't they teach Sam the times tables?

2..

"The road was a ribbon of moonlight over the purple moor,

And the highwayman came riding..."

Henry's strong black tail hit the back of the car seat, *thump, thump, thump, thump,* as Lynn recited "The Highwayman."

He rode with his head out the window. The wind blew his ears straight back so that they pointed toward Chicago. He half closed his eyes to keep out the little specks of dirt that the wind carried along.

He had never been to Indiana before, but he liked the smells already, little peppery smells, and dirt smells, and fresh smells that cooled his nose.

Lynn began to tell Henry about Sam again.

"He's the neatest kid," she said, "and he wants a dog so much. Last week, Dad told me, Sam invented a dog, an Airedale named Rusty. He pretended Rusty was under the dinner table and resting his head on his knee." Lynn drove along, frowning thoughtfully.

"Dad and I both think Sam should have a dog," she added after a while. "But we can't convince Mom. She's sure a dog would dig up her gladiola bulbs."

When Henry had just about decided he couldn't wait any longer to see Little Brother Sam, they turned off the highway and drove through a downtown in which the only light came from the dome of the courthouse. They turned on to a quiet, dark street. In many of the yards, Henry noticed little slanted-roofed dog houses standing in the shadows. Then Lynn drove up a driveway alongside the only lighted porch on the street.

"Yahoo, Henry!" A boy rushed out of a screen door in his pajamas and bare feet. Henry put his front paws on the car door, put his head out the window, and panted impatiently. He wagged his tail right in Lynn's face.

Lynn reached over and opened the car door. Henry bounded out to meet Sam, who threw his arms around Henry's neck and pulled him down to the porch floor. They rolled over and over together. Sam smelled of soap and toothpaste, and Henry got just a little whiff of a toad or frog Sam must have played with that day.

"The porch floor's dirty," Mom said as she hugged Lynn.

Dad pulled Sam away by his pajama top, and Lynn pulled Henry away by his collar.

I like Little Brother Sam, Henry thought.

"You want to know something?" Sam said. "I like Henry."

Dad opened the door and they all went in. "Say hello to your sister and go to bed," Dad told Sam.

Dad's big shoes were heavy, and he smelled of machine oil like the lawn mowers on campus.

Lynn stooped down and hugged Sam. Henry poked his nose between them.

Then Mom said, "Time for bed."

Sam grabbed Henry's collar and pulled him to the stairs.

"You're taking that dog to bed?" Mom asked. "There's a time and place for dogs, and it's not in bed."

Mom smelled nice and wore pretty shoes, but Henry didn't care for the way she talked.

"I gave Henry a bath this morning," Lynn said.

"Aw, Mom," Sam said.

"Oh, all right," Mom said. Henry was surprised. Were the words "Aw, Mom" magic words that he had never learned about?

"I just hope he doesn't shed," Mom continued.

"Hold on to all your hair, Henry," Lynn said, and then laughed. Dad laughed, too, but Mom did not laugh and neither did Henry.

"I just hope he doesn't howl at night," Mom said. "Night is not the time to howl."

"Which reminds me of a little dog poem," Dad said. "I collect poems about dogs," he explained to Henry.

Henry went over and sat down next to Dad. Dad's fingers touched Henry's collar as he stood before his family and recited.

"This is called 'The Dog That Howls at Night,' " Dad said.

"There are canines old and mangy
There are curs that growl and fight
But give me both in preference
To the dog that howls at night."

Again Dad and Lynn broke out into laughter. Mom didn't laugh and neither did Henry. Henry pulled away and ran up the stairs to Sam's room before Mom could change her mind. He knew every room in the house just from listening to Lynn's stories about Indiana.

When Sam and Henry were in bed, Sam pulled the blue quilt all the way over them. It was as if they were in a tent.

"You know what, Henry?" Sam asked. "I wish you could hear me recite 'The Raven' in school tomorrow."

Henry licked Sam's face. He had been waiting for Sam to invite him to Happy Hollow School.

"And want to know something else?" Sam asked. "We made a tepee in our room for our Native American Leaders unit."

Third grade sounded very exciting to Henry. He put his paw on Sam's arm.

Just then Mom, Dad, and Lynn came upstairs to tuck them in.

"Good-night, Sam and Henry," Lynn said. "Now, boys, say good-night to Mom and Dad."

This time it was Mom who laughed. "Imagine me as a dog's mother," she said.

Then she tucked the blue comforter around Sam, gave him a kiss, and said, "It's time for sleep."

After she left, Sam pulled the comforter up around Henry again and threw his arm over him.

"You're my kind of dog," Sam said. "I'm going to tell you about my arithmetic block."

3...

"You see, Henry," Sam said, "the numbers don't like me."

Sam's voice was low in the dark room. Except for his feet, Henry thought, Sam was as warm as a puppy.

"Henry, the numbers are like unfriendly slugs and bugs and spiders with big eyes. There are hundreds and hundreds of them. They never end. You have to shut them out, or they could crawl all over you."

That's going a little far, Henry thought. But it's just as I expected. Sam has closed the door to the number room in his head.

Sam gave a little laugh.

"Not really, of course, Henry. But they *are* unfriendly. ABCs want you to like them, and they get together in good-sounding words like in 'The Raven.' But numbers don't care at all. They're like angry bugs that would just as soon bite you as not, like mosquitoes and ticks and chiggers and fleas."

Henry began to itch all over. He knew about arithmetic blocks all right from Prince, who couldn't count
past two. But a dog could get by without knowing arithmetic. A boy was different. He needed to jingle money

in his pocket, keep baseball scores, and buy treats for his dog.

"I know it sounds funny, Henry, but you know what? My mom works with computers, and I've heard her say she has to get the bugs out of a program."

Henry licked Sam's face.

"You know what, Henry, sometimes my dad'll hold out a nickel, and he'll say, 'See this? Suppose I had four of them, how much would I have? You tell me, and I'll give this nickel to you.' And I'll just stand there and stare at his hand. I can't say a word."

Henry put his paw on Sam's arm. Then he rested his nose against Sam's chin.

"I think I could learn the times tables if I had a dog," Sam said as he fell off to sleep.

Perhaps, Henry thought again. Junior knew his tables through seven. But what if Sam's dog turned out to be like Prince? Then Henry fell asleep, too.

He woke up about an hour later when Mom, Dad, and Lynn came up to bed. They stopped in the lighted hall and looked in on Sam and Henry.

Dad put his arm around Mom. "Isn't it time you forgot about that prize zucchini?"

"It isn't just that," Mom said. "What I can't understand is how come everybody in this family talks to dogs except me. In my family when I was growing up, we would as soon have talked to a fly on the wall."

But, Henry thought, you didn't know a fly on the wall.

14

However, even if Henry had been introduced properly, he would not talk to flies on the wall, or anywhere else. It was disgusting the way they buzzed around the garbage cans at the back door of the Dove Restaurant on Fifty-seventh Street.

"Didn't you ever talk to your dolls, Mom?" Lynn asked.

"Well, I don't talk to them now. You two still talk to dogs even though you're grown up."

"I've seen you talk to babies," Dad said.

"That's different," Mom said, almost fiercely.

"Would you do me a favor this week and think about dogs?" Dad asked. "And then try to understand what a dog can mean to someone?"

"Okay," Mom said. "I'll start tomorrow. I'm taking the afternoon off to go shopping with Lynn, so I'll have plenty of time to think about dogs."

May all your dog thoughts be pleasant ones, Henry wished as he drifted back to sleep.

4....

On Monday morning, everyone left the house together. Sam dawdled behind a little bit, and Henry was able to slip out of the house without anyone noticing. He hoped to return before Lynn and Mom came home from shopping. It was the only way he could get to visit the third grade.

Henry liked walking along with Sam to school. He liked the smells of the rainy Indiana morning, the wet earth, and the cool drops that splashed on his nose.

Suddenly Henry and Sam were surrounded by boys and girls all about the same size as Sam. They ran and yelled and dropped their books. They skipped backward and threw a soccer ball at one another. Henry's tail wagged so hard it began to go around in a circle.

Lucy Marie patted Henry. She had freckles and smelled of Winesap apples.

"I wish we could take Henry into school with us," she said.

"I don't think Mrs. Hanson would allow it," Sam said as he jumped into a puddle. "Even though Henry goes to college classes with my sister, Lynn."

"Really? Maybe he'd be bored at Happy Hollow School," Lucy Marie said.

"No, no, no!" Henry barked loudly, afraid they wouldn't understand.

Nathan walked along, balancing his notebook on his head. "We could keep him in the tepee," he said.

"Yes, yes," Henry barked.

He jumped up and put his feet on Nathan's chest. Nathan sat down without meaning to, his legs straight out in front of him. His papers went everywhere. Then Henry stood with his front paws on Nathan's knees and licked his face. Nathan smelled of peanut butter and chocolate milk.

"I think Henry wants to go to school," Sam said.

"That settles it," Lucy Marie said. "We'll take him."

Lucy Marie stooped down and hugged Henry, putting her face against his. Henry had thought her freckles might scratch, but it turned out her face was as smooth as a puppy's stomach.

When Lucy Marie got up, Sam stooped down and hugged Henry, too. "I don't know how you can stand to have a girl hug you," he whispered.

They made their plans.

Lucy Marie would go into the schoolroom first. As soon as Mrs. Hanson, their teacher, went to the office to collect her mail and the morning announcements, Lucy Marie would go to the window and wave her red scarf at Sam and Nathan. Then Henry would walk into the room surrounded by Sam and Nathan and all their friends. They would put him in the tepee and cover him with their raincoats.

"But can he keep quiet?" Nathan asked.

Henry barked and jumped up on Nathan. Nathan's notebook fell off his head again.

"If he can keep quiet at those boring talks at college, he can keep quiet in the third grade," Sam promised. This time he helped Nathan pick his wet papers up.

5

Henry walked quietly among the children. For the first time in his life he wished he were not such a black dog with such a shiny black dog's coat. It was a good thing that the sun wasn't out, or his coat would have picked up glints almost like a mirror. After a few steps, Sam took off his dull tan raincoat and put it over Henry, with the hood over Henry's head and the sleeves hanging down on the sides. Henry felt very silly. But he would stand a lot worse to find out what went on in Happy Hollow Elementary School.

At last they were in the room. Nathan and Sam hurried Henry over to the tepee. Their friends covered him with more raincoats. Lucy Marie put the cuff of the sleeve of her coat at the opening of the tepee, and then she showed Henry how he could put his nose into the sleeve through the shoulder and peek out the opening of the tepee.

Then all the children ran to their desks, picked up their books, and started to read, even though the bell had not yet rung. They didn't want Mrs. Hanson to look at the tepee.

Mrs. Hanson walked into the room clearing her throat,

preparing to call out above the noise and bustle. She glanced at them in surprise.

"What a fine group of boys and girls I have here!" she said. "This must be the best grade in our whole school."

Sam shuffled his feet. Nathan blushed. Lucy Marie licked her lips. Then the bell rang and school began. What a morning it was!

The first lesson was reading. Henry lay quietly and listened. But then Sam read. He did it so beautifully that Henry forgot where he was. His tail wagged.

Thump, thump, thump, thump.

Nathan jumped up from his seat and stamped his foot on the floor. "Excuse me, Mrs. Hanson," he said. "This helps if your foot goes to sleep."

Henry was embarrassed. He had never thumped his tail on the floor in college. He made up his mind that his tail would lie still no matter what.

All went well for the next half hour while the class discussed why they should eat many vegetables and not much candy. I believe the same must be true for dogs, Henry thought sleepily.

Henry was warm in the tepee and he could hear the rain outside. I feel like Hiawatha, he thought. He began to get sleepy. Luckily Henry did not snore.

He woke up with a start to hear, "Once upon a midnight dreary. . . ." He looked out through the sleeve.

Sam stood up straight in front of the classroom, with his hands down at his sides. He was reciting "The Raven."

Henry wanted to chime in with Sam. Instead he said the words under his breath. But when he heard the words "Quoth the Raven, 'Nevermore,' " his tail could not restrain itself.

Thump, thump, thump, thump.

Lucy Marie began to hit her table with a book.

"Sorry, Mrs. Hanson," she said, "I had to applaud."

The teacher looked puzzled.

Henry lay quietly for the rest of the poem. After Sam had returned to his seat, he waved his hand.

"What is it, Sam?" Mrs. Hanson asked.

"I know you're going to think this is funny, Mrs. Hanson," Sam said. "But could we have our number drill sitting in front of the tepee, just as Native American boys and girls did in the old days?"

Mrs. Hanson looked like a grown-up Lucy Marie, but she had more skin between each freckle.

"I don't know if Native American boys and girls had number drills in the old days," she said. "But if it will help your arithmetic, Sam, I'm all for it."

The class sat down on the floor in front of the tepee. Sam sat near the entrance. He reached in under the coats and put his hand on Henry's tail, which was curled up alongside Henry.

Now Henry was going to see Sam's arithmetic block in action.

6

"Sam," Mrs. Hanson said, "how much is one times two?"

She smiled at him. Henry knew she was hoping to make the numbers seem friendly. He approved. She had asked Sam the easiest number problem in the world.

But Sam began to shake. He squeezed Henry's tail so hard it hurt, and his hand was cold and sweaty at the same time. Henry knew he had come face-to-face (or hand to tail) with Sam's arithmetic block. He wanted to help Sam so much that he twitched his tail two times in Sam's hand.

"Two?" Sam asked.

"Very good," Mrs. Hanson said.

But instead of relaxing his hold on Henry's tail, Sam began to hold on tighter and tighter as Mrs. Hanson went around the room asking harder and harder problems. An arithmetic block was no joke! Both Sam and Henry were glad when she asked Nathan nine times nine. That would have been a lot of tail wags. Sam squeezed Henry's tail so tight that Henry yelped—a small yelp, but a yelp nevertheless.

Lucy put her hand on her stomach.

"Oh . . . oo," she cried.

"Lucy Marie, are you sick?" Mrs. Hanson asked.

Lucy Marie leaned her head to one side toward the tepee, listening. Henry was quiet. Sam had stopped squeezing Henry's tail.

"I'm okay now, Mrs. Hanson," Lucy said.

"Good," Mrs. Hanson said. "Now Sam, can you tell me how much three times one is?"

Such easy problems, Henry thought. But still Sam shook. Henry could not stand having Sam suffer like that. He wagged his tail three times in Sam's hand.

"Three," Sam said.

"Very good," said Mrs. Hanson in a surprised voice. "How much is four times one?"

This time Sam shouted without even raising his hand. "Four."

"You are doing fine, Sam. How much is two times two?"

Henry flapped his tail four times.

"Four!" Sam shouted again.

"This is a day of wonders," Mrs. Hanson said.

The whole class smiled at Sam.

"Your arithmetic block is gone!" Lucy Marie said to Sam.

"Let me shake your hand," Nathan told him.

Sam took his right hand out of the tepee to shake Nathan's hand.

"How much is three times two?" Mrs. Hanson asked.

Thump, thump, thump, thump, thump, thump.

Sam had forgotten to hold Henry's tail.

All the boys and girls who had brought Henry into the room started to hit the floor with their hands.

"We're like Native Americans hitting tom-toms," Lucy Marie said, "to celebrate Sam's breaking his arithmetic block."

Henry saw Mrs. Hanson point to the tepee. "What was that thumping?" she asked. "It seemed to come from there."

"What thumping?" Sam asked.

Mrs. Hanson got up from her chair. She stooped down and pulled the flap of the tepee all the way open. Henry lay very quietly under the coats.

"What are all those coats doing there on the floor?" she asked.

"Don't worry, Mrs. Hanson. I'll pick them up at recess," Nathan said.

"Maybe in the old days Native American boys and girls threw their raincoats on the floor," Lucy Marie said.

Everybody's neck and face got red then. Even Mrs. Hanson seemed embarrassed by Lucy Marie's idea. She was still looking at the tepee.

"Oh, well," she said, and sat down again. "You pick up

every coat when the bell rings," she said to Nathan. Then she looked back at the tepee again.

"Theirs not to reason why . . ."

She said those words more to herself than to the class. She often said those words, and the class always knew that when she said them, everything was going to be all right.

But the words were from Henry's favorite poem. He could keep still no longer. She was his kind of teacher, and he had to let her know it. He jumped out from under the coats, almost knocking Mrs. Hanson over. He licked her face.

"Help!" Mrs. Hanson screamed.

"My sister's dog . . ." "He's just . . ." "We thought . . ."

Mrs. Hanson listened for a few minutes while all the children tried to tell the story at once.

Finally she said, "Quiet. I want to think."

She put her hand to her head and went to sit down at her desk. The children went back to their seats and sat very still. Henry lay next to Sam's desk. His tail didn't even quiver. Mrs. Hanson's face began to smooth out, and the children felt better. Then Mrs. Hanson frowned again.

"But what about those arithmetic answers, Sam?"

Confusion broke out again while Sam tried to explain. Only Henry was calm.

"If you can keep your head when all about you
Are losing theirs and blaming it on you . . ."

Henry recited the whole poem to himself while he waited.

Mrs. Hanson sat with her hand to her head. She didn't look up for a whole minute.

"Sam," she said at last with a sigh, "you take the dog home now. It's almost time for recess."

Sam's baseball team missed him at recess, but all in all the class felt that things could have been worse. For Sam, however, something very important had happened.

7.

Sam came into the house after school, whistling. If he had a tail, he'd be wagging it, Henry thought.

Sam grabbed a box of cookies in one hand and Henry's collar in the other. Then he took Henry out to his secret hiding place under the willow tree in the backyard, where the branches went all the way to the ground.

"Henry, I'm going to tell you something. I've been thinking about this all afternoon. It was fun having the right answers for once in arithmetic, but I couldn't carry you to arithmetic every day. You're too big."

And Mrs. Hanson would never allow it, Henry thought. But he waited. He could tell there was more to come.

"But we have to figure out a way for me to get the right answers. You know why? I've been telling Mom that if I had a dog I could do arithmetic. We have to prove it by Saturday, because that's when you're going home."

Henry agreed with everything Sam said.

"What if you and I brainstorm like my dad does at

work? I'll give you ideas off the top of my head, and you wag your tail when you think I have a good one."

Henry wagged his tail.

"Oh, and Henry, you know all that stuff about numbers being fleas? Forget it. I figure if a dog doesn't worry about numbers being fleas, why should I?"

Henry was impressed. Sam had looked his fears in the eye and said good-bye to them.

Sam sat down and faced Henry.

"Okay, Henry. How about if I borrowed a tiny dog and a big briefcase? I'd put him in so that just his tail stuck out and he could wag out the answers for me in class."

Henry's tail didn't even quiver.

"You're right, Henry," Sam said. "Besides, Mrs. Hanson won't even let us bring the tiniest calculators into class. She says the tables have to be inside our heads."

Sam began to bring ideas forth so fast that Henry became dizzy.

"Suppose I copied the times tables down on a sheet of paper and then ate it?"

Henry felt a little sick. It would be better to bake the tables into a cookie. But he didn't really think the way to Sam's head was through his stomach.

"Suppose I recorded the tables and played the tape under my pillow at night?"

Henry felt a little twitch in his tail. That might be worth a try—if they had all the time in the world.

"This is a good one, Henry. I'll empty my mind, and you think the table of twos as hard as you can. We'll try to move it from your head into mine."

Henry wagged his tail. He would like to be able to move thoughts from his head to Sam's, or to Lynn's. He would like to let Lynn know that on June eighteenth, the anniversary of the day they found each other, he wanted chicken divan with oven-browned potatoes for dinner.

Sam closed his eyes and put his arms around Henry's neck. Henry lay down next to Sam and said the twos table in his head. After he had said it three times, he sat up.

Sam slowly opened his eyes. Henry waited for him to speak.

"Henry, not one number came into my head. Not a single one. All I could think of was how I'd like chicken divan with oven-browned potatoes for my birthday dinner."

It wasn't that the plan was bad, Henry thought. It was that it would take them too long to work it out.

Sam was quiet for a few minutes, his face screwed up in thought. "I can think of only one other way," he said finally.

Henry knew what the way was, and he was sorry, too.

"We have to face it," Sam said. "I'm going to have to memorize the tables. I'm going to have to memorize them all this week. Will you help me?"

Henry wagged his tail.

"I'm going to keep it a secret from everyone but you.

Nobody else is going to know about it until I finish the nines table."

Henry nestled his nose next to Sam's neck to show his approval.

"Every day between four and six, I'm going to close my eyes and memorize." Sam still looked determined.

Henry lifted up his paw to shake hands on the deal.

"I'll begin tomorrow, no matter what happens," Sam said. "Now, Henry, help me with my homework. It's only a few little problems, and then we'll have time to play."

At dinnertime that night, Henry lay under the table.

"This is great, Mom," Lynn said.

"Have some mashed potatoes and gravy," Mom said. "And I made bread for you."

"I can smell it," Lynn said.

"There's strawberry shortcake for dessert."

"I could just die," Lynn said. "Everything is so good."

"I'm not talking," Dad said. "I'm eating."

"Me, too," Sam mumbled.

"Don't talk with your mouth full," Mom said happily.

The whole family stopped talking, and all Henry heard was the scraping of knives and forks across their plates. Every so often Lynn or Sam would pass down a delicious tidbit to him. Then he heard them push their chairs out from the table and groan in different voices.

Outside it began to rain again.

"Sam," Dad said sternly.

"Yes, Dad?" Sam said.

"Isn't this your night for arithmetic homework?"

"I did it," Sam said quietly.

Dad didn't hear him.

"There's no TV for you until you do it."

"I did it," Sam said again, a little louder.

But Dad wasn't listening. One of his feet was tapping on the floor. Henry would have liked to put his paw on it to stop it.

"I'll help you," Dad said, "if you'll work, too. But I won't do it for you."

"But, Dad," Sam said. "I *did* it."

Dad had worked himself up.

"You've got to learn," Dad said, "that . . ." He stopped. "What did you say?"

"He did it," Mom and Lynn shouted.

"I did it," Sam shouted.

"He did it," Henry barked.

Sam ran and got his workbook to show Dad.

"I can't believe it," Dad said. "You did it all by yourself?"

"Well, not exactly," Sam said, sounding a little embarrassed. "Henry helped me." He pulled Henry out from under the table.

"Good," Dad said, and nothing more. As Henry looked at the faces of Mom, Dad, and Lynn, he realized no one believed Sam, not even Lynn.

8

On Tuesday afternoon, when Sam came home from school, he found an envelope taped to the cookie box. Inside was a grocery list, five dollars, and a note from Lynn that read, "Will you get these things for Mom? I'm studying at the library. Thanks. See you at dinner."

After Sam and Henry finished their cookies and milk, they started out to the store. "It's fun going on errands when you have a dog," Sam said. Henry wagged his tail.

But on the way there Sam's alarm watch started to beep.

Sam took out a card from his pocket, glanced at it, closed his eyes and began, "One times one equals one, one times one equals one." He stepped off the curb. Henry looked to the left. A motorcycle came roaring toward Sam. The driver wore a black helmet, and he had a tennis racket slung over his shoulder.

Henry grabbed Sam's belt in his teeth and pulled him

back so hard that Sam sat down on the curb.

Sam opened his eyes, and they both coughed in the dust left by the motorcycle. When its roar had faded into a hum, Sam turned to Henry. "You saved my life, Henry! You'd better lead from now on. Just pretend you're a Seeing Eye dog." Sam took hold of Henry's collar. "Wait until Mom hears this."

Henry had always admired Seeing Eye dogs. He thought they worked in the noblest profession a dog could have.

The door to the Village Pantry was open. The clerk was at the cash register.

"What can I do for you?" the clerk said as Henry led Sam in. "One times nine equals nine, one times nine equals nine," Sam said as he put the list down on the counter. He kept his eyes closed.

"Well, I never." But the clerk very nicely took the list. She brought back the milk, butter, and bread and laid them on the counter. Henry put his nose into Sam's pocket and brought out the five-dollar bill, which he placed on the counter.

"Well, I never," the clerk said again.

"One times nine equals nine," Sam said.

She put the items in the bag and came around to put the change into Sam's pocket.

"It's good to see a boy who's caught up in his studies. Take good care of him, doggie."

Henry licked her hand. "One times nine equals nine,"

Sam repeated as they left the store. By dinnertime, Sam knew the tables of ones, twos, and threes.

"Mom is really going to change her mind about dogs when she finds out you saved my life," Sam told Henry as they went into dinner.

But dinner wasn't as pleasant that night as it had been the night before. The food was good. They had grilled catfish and green beans and baked apples. Henry enjoyed each bite Lynn and Sam passed under the table to him. But Mom thought that Henry had broken two tulip stalks.

"With all the moles, possums, raccoons, squirrels, stray dogs, little children, and goodness knows who else comes into this yard, why blame Henry?" Dad said.

"I know what I know," Mom said.

"Talk about faulty generalizations, Mom," Lynn said.

"By the way, Mom," Sam said, "Henry saved my life today."

"Is that so?" Dad said doubtfully. "How did he do that?"

"I had my eyes closed when we came to Jefferson Street, and he pulled me back by my belt just as a motorcycle doing one hundred miles an hour at least came straight at me."

"Why were your eyes closed?" Dad asked.

"We were playing that Henry was a Seeing Eye dog."

"Really, Sam!" Dad said sternly.

Lynn just laughed and petted Sam and Henry at the same time. "Let's watch the White Sox game tonight, guys," she said.

It was clear to Henry that the family hadn't believed Sam again. Was this getting to be a habit? What would they refuse to believe tomorrow?

On Wednesday afternoon, Henry was lying under the old maple tree in the backyard, sleepily watching a wood-pecker drill a hole in the trunk, when Sam opened the gate.

"Come on, Henry," he called. "The baseball game starts in five minutes."

Henry pricked up his ears. He was very good at catching balls.

"We're going to play the Golden Eagles. That's the other third-grade class. We're the Pumas. It's our last game and so far we're tied," Sam explained. "You have to help us, Henry!"

Maybe they'll let me be catcher, Henry thought as they ran up to school. He would like to stand behind the plate and give signals to the pitcher. He could scratch the dust with his paws and walk to the pitcher's mound, maybe even eat a hot dog on the bench.

But the team had different plans for Henry.

"Your first job is to baby-sit the kindergartners," Sam said when they got to the playground. "They have to wait for the players to take them home."

The captain of the other team, the Golden Eagles, had twin brothers in kindergarten. He took charge.

"Listen, you guys," he said to them, "You stick close to Henry or I'll pound you." Then he passed out lollipops and bubble gum to all of them.

They stuck close to Henry all right. Besides being the

shortest people Henry had ever met, they were also the stickiest. Their red cheeks, sweet-smelling and tasting of strawberry, cherry, and orange, stuck to Henry when they hugged him. One bubble broke right on Henry's ear.

Each time they petted him, which was often, their hands stuck to his fur. But Henry liked them. They were like puppies, and they tasted so good.

Sam came over and put his head close to Henry's. "I haven't forgotten about the times tables. I'm going to play right field. Nobody ever hits out there. When my alarm goes off, I'll close my eyes and memorize the fours and fives tables. If a ball really *is* coming out to me, you bark."

Henry had a hard time wagging his tail, because a kindergartner was standing on it.

Sam's team was up first. Nathan got a hit. "Rah, rah, Nathan," the kindergartners yelled. Lucy Marie got a hit. "Rah, rah, Lucy Marie," they yelled. Sam hit a home run and the kindergartners went wild. "Rah, rah, rah, Sam!"

At the end of the first inning the score was three to two in favor of Sam's team. The kindergartners had cheered the players on the other side, too. They didn't know about teams. They just cheered every time a player got a hit, and the only cheer they knew was *rah rah*.

Sam's alarm went off in the second inning, while he was out in right field. He took a look at a card, closed his eyes, and began, "Four times one equals four." Henry pushed his nose past the kindergartners in front of him to watch the batters. Sam had been right. They didn't seem to hit the ball anywhere near right field.

In the fourth inning, instead of joining his team on the bench, Sam sat down with Henry and the kindergartners so that he could work on his times tables.

He closed his eyes. "Four times two equals eight, four times two equals eight," he said as Nathan went up to bat. Nathan got a hit. "Four times two equals eight," Sam said.

"Four times two equals eight, four times two equals eight, four times two equals eight, Nathan, Nathan, rah, rah, rah," the kindergartners said. They thought *four times two equals eight* was a new cheer.

Henry nudged Sam with his nose when it was his turn to bat.

Sam got a two-bagger. The kindergartners yelled, "Four times two equals eight, four times two equals eight, rah, rah, Sam!"

Sam didn't come back to sit with them again. He said the bench was quieter.

It was a close game. By the bottom of the ninth the score was fifteen to fourteen in favor of Sam's team. The other third-grade team was up to bat. Two players had already struck out, and one was on second base.

Sam was in right field. His eyes were closed. "Five times five equals twenty-five, five times five equals twenty-five," he said.

The littlest girl on the Golden Eagles team came up to bat.

"It's in the bag," yelled Nathan. "She hasn't had a hit all season."

Sam's team was cheering already. The kindergartners were tumbling all over Henry, yelling "Four times two equals eight, four times two equals eight."

Henry saw Nathan wind up. He saw him throw the ball. He watched the curve of the ball and the girl at bat. His eyes were good, and he'd watched plenty of White Sox games that season. Henry knew it was going to be a hit before the bat even touched the ball. He jumped up so quickly the kindergartners fell off him.

Thwack!

Henry barked and ran out to right field at the same time, in case Sam couldn't hear him. The kindergartners yelled, "Four times two equals eight, four times two equals eight," and followed Henry out to right field.

Sam opened his eyes just in time to see the ball sail over his head. He tried to back up, his glove in the air to catch the ball, but he bumped into two kindergartners. They all fell to the ground in a heap. "Oh, no!" Sam groaned.

But Henry had run behind Sam, looking over his shoulder and watching the ball all the time. He twisted around, leaped up, and picked the ball right out of the air with his mouth.

"We won," Nathan yelled.

"*We* won," the Golden Eagles yelled.

"Henry won," the kindergartners shouted.

There was a very long argument. By the time it was over, Sam had reached five times seven equals thirty-five.

The Golden Eagles said that Henry was not a member of the Pumas' team and therefore his catch shouldn't count and their hit *should* count. If the hit were counted, they would win because both the player on second base and the hitter would have scored. The score would be sixteen to fifteen in favor of the Golden Eagles.

But the Pumas said there had been too many kindergartners out in right field for Sam to get to the ball. "Besides that," Nathan said, "more of the kindergartners belong to your team than to ours."

They called on the third-grade teachers to decide. Mrs. Hanson whispered with the other third-grade teacher, Mrs. Conti, for a long time. Then Mrs. Conti nodded.

"When does Henry go home?" Mrs. Hanson asked.

"On Saturday," Sam said sadly.

"The game will be replayed on Monday," Mrs. Hanson said.

"I'll bring cookies for everybody," Mrs. Conti added.

Such decisiveness, Henry thought. They should have jobs in the American League.

By dinnertime, Sam had memorized the fives table. "How did your game go?" Dad asked.

"It was sort of tied," Sam said. "We have to play it again next Monday."

Then Sam added in a very quiet voice, "Henry made a great catch."

Henry didn't know if anyone else had heard Sam. He didn't think so. No one congratulated Henry. No one said a word.

9

Nathan's older brother, David, had promised to take Nathan and Sam fishing down at the Wabash River on Thursday afternoon. Henry tagged along.

When Sam's alarm went off at four o'clock, he got up and pointed to a sycamore tree farther down the river.

"I'm going to try over there for a while. You can see me from here. Come on, Henry."

"Well, don't go any farther. I promised your mom I'd keep an eye on you," said David, who was in high school.

When it came time to go home, David had caught three catfishes and two bluegills. Nathan had two bluegills and one catfish. Sam hadn't caught a single fish.

"You want my catfish?" Nathan asked him.

"No thanks," Sam said.

"That spot you chose to fish in was good for nothing," David said.

It might have helped if Sam had put some bait on his

line, Henry thought. I think it makes the fish angry to see an empty hook.

"It was good for something," Sam whispered to Henry. "I learned the sixes and sevens tables."

At four o'clock on Friday, Sam and Henry went out to the secret hiding place under the willow tree. It started to sprinkle, but they were as dry as if they were in the house, at least at first. They got through the eights table, which Sam had been dreading, and came to what seemed to be the hardest job of all: the nines table.

"Nothing for it but to jump right in," Sam said.

Sam's attitude toward arithmetic had certainly changed, thought Henry proudly.

"Guess what?" Sam said, going through his pockets. "I lost my card with the nines table on it. This is going to take longer than we thought if you have to wag out all the answers with your tail. Except I know nine times one," Sam said. "That's nine."

He took a stick and wrote 9 in the dirt.

"You know what?" Sam said. "It's the same as one times nine."

That's because multiplication is commutative, Henry thought.

"Do you think it's the same with the others, Henry? Do they all go backward and forward like that?"

Henry wagged his tail hard and breathed a big sigh of relief. He was sure Mrs. Hanson had told the class that many times. But that was when Sam had been afraid numbers were going to bite him and had kept the doors and windows of the arithmetic room in his head locked against them.

Sam took a stick and wrote the nines table in the dirt slowly. He figured out all the answers except one. "Now I just have to memorize them. That's easy. But what do I do about nine times nine?"

Henry wagged his tail.

"You're a good friend, Henry," Sam said.

It began to rain harder as Sam memorized. Henry fell asleep while Sam was saying nine times four equals thirty-six. He woke up when Sam tugged at his ear.

"Henry," he said, "I've reached nine times nine."

Eighty-one wags of Henry's tail! He hoped his tail was up to it.

It was going to be a hard job for Sam, too. They both had to count as Henry wagged.

"Whatever happens, don't stop," Sam said. "Because we'll have to start all over again."

Just when Henry reached twenty-seven, he heard Mom say, "Lynn, I don't know where Sam is, and there's a real storm coming up." Henry peeked through the willow branches, still wagging. Mom was standing on the porch, looking worried.

Henry kept wagging and Sam kept counting. Every so often the branches that went all the way to the ground would blow aside, and Henry would see all the trees in the yard bending over. Even the big old maple tree with all the birds' nests in it was swaying, and the wind blew harder each second.

When they reached forty-seven, the willow branches swept all the way to the side, and Mom saw them from the porch. "There they are, under the willow tree. Sam, come in this minute!"

Henry nudged Sam and they got up. Sam walked slowly, holding on to Henry's tail. He didn't want to lose count.

"Sixty-six, sixty-seven, sixty-eight—"

"Hurry up," Mom said. "You're getting soaked."

"Seventy, seventy-one, seventy-two," Sam said, still with his eyes closed. They were already soaked. There didn't seem much reason to hurry.

Henry couldn't believe how far the big maple tree was swaying. The rain clouds were so low that the top twigs seemed to scrape right across them.

"Seventy-nine, eighty—"

Henry heard Mom scream. The whole giant maple tree swayed up ahead as if it were a sapling, and it kept on going! The maple tree was falling down!

Henry whirled around and jumped on Sam. He stumbled backward and opened his eyes in surprise. Henry jumped again and knocked Sam right off his feet. He stood on top of him.

Crash! The tree hit the ground. The whole yard shook. A giant hole had appeared where the maple tree once

stood. The tree stretched in front of them, a bird's nest still tangled in the upper branches.

"Wow," Sam said, sitting up. "Would you look at that tree?"

"Sam! Sam!" Mom and Lynn called.

"We're here," Sam yelled. "Quick, Henry." He grabbed Henry's tail.

Henry wagged it one more time and stopped.

"Is it eighty-one? Does nine times nine equal eighty-one?" Sam asked.

Henry stamped his paw to show he'd finished, just as Mom and Lynn ran around the big hole where the maple tree once stood to reach them.

"I'll never forget it," Sam whispered to Henry.

I hope Mom doesn't think I knocked down the maple tree, Henry thought.

10

The maple tree had fallen down just as Dad had turned into the driveway. Now, he kept looking from Mom to Lynn to Sam as if he were counting them over and over again to make sure they were all there. Then he would look at Henry and say, "Good dog."

Mom was drying Henry off with her thickest towel. Henry loved it.

"You saved Sam's life," Mom said. "Will you ever forgive me?"

Henry could smell chicken divan and oven-browned potatoes in the oven. He could forgive anyone who cooked like Mom.

He was trying to transfer a thought to Sam. Ask your parents for a dog, Sam. Now's the time. Get a promise. Get a promise. Get a promise.

"Now can I have a dog?" Sam said.

"You can have any dog in the world," Mom said as if she were a queen.

"Any dog?" Sam asked. He looked over to Henry.

Thoughts were flying around the room.

Henry, Dad, and Lynn knew what Sam had in his mind. They all looked worried. Lynn looked sick. She moved close to Henry, took the towel out of Mom's hand, and started drying him.

"As long as he doesn't belong to anyone else," she said.

"Oh, Sam knows that," Dad said.

But Sam didn't look as if he did. He looked as if he were about to cry.

So did Lynn. But her chin was out.

"Henry's mine," Lynn said. "I'll never give him up."

She said it very firmly. Of course not, Henry thought. They had chosen each other. Lynn needed him. Who else could walk her home from the library at night and listen to her recite poetry?

"But I'll bring him to visit you and your dog," Lynn promised. "Henry can teach him lots of things."

Sam looked even sadder.

"Lynn . . . ," Mom said. "Maybe you could visit Henry here on weekends?" Henry could tell that Mom still didn't understand fully about dogs.

"No," Lynn said. "He's mine. He belongs with me. Henry can be Sam's dog's big brother."

Sam was quiet.

"He can come to visit, and sometimes you'll have two dogs to play with," Dad said.

"He can teach your dog about baseball. He can give him advice," Lynn said.

"And you can read and recite poems to him," Dad added.

"You can get a puppy. No one should miss having a puppy in his life," Lynn said. "When a little puppy goes down a stair, he leaps out into space instead of stepping down."

She ran for her purse and took out some pictures of Henry as a puppy. "See? Look how the grass comes up to his knees."

I *was* pretty cute, Henry thought.

Sam smiled for the first time.

"Tomorrow, before Lynn leaves, we can all go out to the kennel, and Henry can help you pick out a puppy," Mom said.

"And Henry can teach Rusty the times tables," Sam said.

"Who's Rusty?" Mom asked.

"You know the greatest boy in the world?" Dad asked. "Rusty's his dog."

While Mom got dinner on the table, Lynn put a tape in the stereo. Dad went over and took Mom by the hand, and they did some old dance called the Twist. Henry began to dance, too. He turned round and round, smelling the chicken divan on the stove, the lilacs from the open window, and the apple cider on the table.

"Come on, Sam!" Lynn said, joining in. Sam got up and started to dance, too. Everybody danced separately, but together.

When, at last, they started to sit down at the table, Dad said, "Who are all those little children on our front porch?"

Sam ran to the door. Five kindergartners stood on the porch with the captain of the Golden Eagles.

"They want to say good-bye to Henry," he explained.

"Four times two equals eight, four times two equals eight, Henry, Henry, rah, rah, rah!" the kindergartners cheered.

"Henry caught the ball," one of the twins said.

"Naturally. I believe it," Dad said. "He helped Sam with his homework, too."

"Can Henry come to our birthday party on June fifteenth?" the other twin asked.

Henry wagged his tail. He knew he and Lynn would visit Indiana again before summer school began. He put out his paw to show them he accepted. He licked the twins' cheeks. They tasted of strawberry.

Finally, after the kindergartners left, they all sat down to dinner. It was a wonderful dinner, with even Mom passing tidbits down to Henry from the table.

Henry would have liked to compliment Mom. He wanted her to know that the food she cooked was even better than the scraps that fell out of the garbage cans behind the Dove Restaurant.

"You know what?" Sam said at the end of the meal. "Rusty's going to need a dog house."

"You're right," Dad said, "and that reminds me of a dog poem." He stood up in his place.

"This poem is called 'Motto for a Dog House.'

"I love this little house because
    It offers after dark,
A pause for rest, a rest for paws,
    A place to moor my bark."

Everyone clapped and laughed.

Then Sam got to his feet. "I have something to recite, too."

Sam walked to the center of the kitchen. He stood very straight before his family, his hands down at his sides. He looked at Henry.

He began, "One times one equals one, one times two equals two . . ."

You could have heard a leaf turn. Everybody sat there listening, holding their breath. No one moved as Sam recited.

"Nine times nine equals eighty-one," Sam finished at last.

For a moment everyone sat still, not quite believing what they had heard. Mom and Dad had tears in their eyes. Then they all rushed to Sam. Henry was there first, licking Sam's face with kisses of congratulation.

It will never be quite the same, Henry thought. He was even a bit jealous of Rusty. But then he thought, Now I'll have a little brother in Indiana, too—just like Lynn.

About the Poems

Sam and Lynn's family like these poems because they are fun to read and fun to say.

The line quoted by Lynn on page 6 is from "The Highwayman" (1906) by Alfred Noyes. The highwayman is a robber who visits a landlord's daughter, even though the British soldiers are watching for him. It's an exciting and musical poem.

"The Dog That Howls at Night" by Herbert J. Bryce, which Dad recites on page 10, was published by *The Rotarian* in January 1942 and appears by permission of the magazine.

On pages 22–23, Sam quotes two lines from "The Raven" (1845) by Edgar Allan Poe. In this poem, a raven comes into a man's chamber one midnight, perches above the door, and keeps saying, "Nevermore." (Sam and Henry like this poem more for its sound than its meaning.)

Mrs. Hanson quotes part of a line from "The Charge of the Light Brigade" (1845) by Alfred, Lord Tennyson on page 29. It is a poem about six hundred soldiers who charge into a hopeless battle just because their commander orders them to. The line Mrs. Hanson quotes from is the most famous line in the poem.

Later on page 29, Henry comforts himself with lines from "If" (1910) by Rudyard Kipling. "If" became famous because of its advice to boys on how to become worthwhile men. Perhaps the reader's grandfather or great-grandfather tried to follow this advice.

Dad recites another dog poem on page 59, "Motto for a Dog House" by Arthur Guiterman. The poem first appeared in *Wildwood Fables* and is reprinted by permission of Louise H. Sclove.